Howard B. Wigglebottom

Learns About Courage

Howard Binkow

Reverend Ana

Jeremy Norton

Howard Binkow
Reverend Ana
Illustration by Jeremy Norton
Special thanks to Warren Muzak
Book design by Jane Darroch Riley

Thunderbolt Publishing
We Do Listen Foundation
www.wedolisten.org

Thunderbolt Publishing
We Do Listen Foundation
www.wedolisten.org

Gratitude and appreciation are given to all those who reviewed the story prior to publication;
the book became much better by incorporating several of their suggestions:

Teachers, librarians, counselors and students at:

Bossier Parish Schools, Bossier City, Louisiana
Chalker Elementary, Kennesaw, Georgia
Charleston Elementary, Charleston, Arkansas
Cummings Elementary School, Misawa Air Force Base, Japan
Forest Avenue Elementary, Hudson, Massachusetts
Garden Elementary, Venice, Florida
Glen Alpine Elementary, Morganton, North Carolina
Golden West Elementary, Manteca, California
Hartsdale Avenue Public School, Mississauga, Ontario, Canada

Iveland Elementary School, St. Louis, Missouri
Kincaid Elementary, Marietta, Georgia
Lamarque Elementary School, North Port, Florida
Lee Elementary, Los Alamitos, California
Sherman Oaks Elementary, Sherman Oaks, California
Victoria Avenue Elementary, South Gate, California
Walt Disney Magnet School, Chicago, Illinois
West Navarre Primary, Navarre, Florida

Printed September 2012

Printed in Malaysia by Tien Wah Press (Pte) Limited.

ISBN 978-0-9826165-7-4

LCCN 2012938875

This book belongs to

_____

Nobody knew why Howard B. Wigglebottom had been so afraid the past few weeks. He just wasn't himself. He was scared of the dark and what could be under his bed...

... he was scared of toilets, loud noises and high places. He crossed the street whenever he saw strange people and dogs.

He stopped playing
outside altogether
because of the
possibility of
seeing spiders
and snakes.

But most of all he
feared the first day
at school.

7

When he decided not to leave his room ever again, his friends and family became very worried.

One morning when he was looking outside the window he saw a baby bird looking in.

"Are you here to watch my important moment?" asked the bird.

"It's my first day of learning how to fly."

"Oh! How are you going to do that?" asked Howard.
"I thought all birds were born knowing how to fly."
"No, no, we learn only after we jump out of the nest,"
answered the bird.

"You don't even know if you can fly and you jump anyway?
Aren't you afraid?" asked Howard.
"Yes, we get butterflies in our tummies from fear that our
wings might not work–but we do it anyway." said the bird.
"Watch me. Here I go."

"Wait!!" Howard said. "Should I place something under the tree?" But before he could finish his question, the little bird jumped out of it's nest.

"I did it! I did it! Look how high I can go!" said the bird. Howard was amazed.
The bird was such a fast learner–and so BRAVE too...

"I wish I could be more like you," said Howard. "Lately I am so afraid of everything–not sure what's wrong with me."

"My mother says everybody is afraid of something," said the bird. "The reason we have fears is to learn about courage. If we are not afraid of anything we can't have courage."

"So all superheroes are brave because they have fear but do what they have to do anyway?" asked Howard.

"Yes," said the bird, "If you're not afraid, you can't be BRAVE."

Howard liked the idea. Birds and superheroes were afraid but that didn't stop them from doing what they wanted to do.
He could try that too!

That night he smiled at the dark and the make-believe monsters and told himself, "It's OK to be afraid." He slept well all night! When he woke up he decided to do the things he liked to do even if he was afraid. He wanted to get ready for his biggest fear, the first day at his new school.

He listened to loud noises and it was OK. "I'm brave. I was afraid but I did it anyway," Howard told himself.

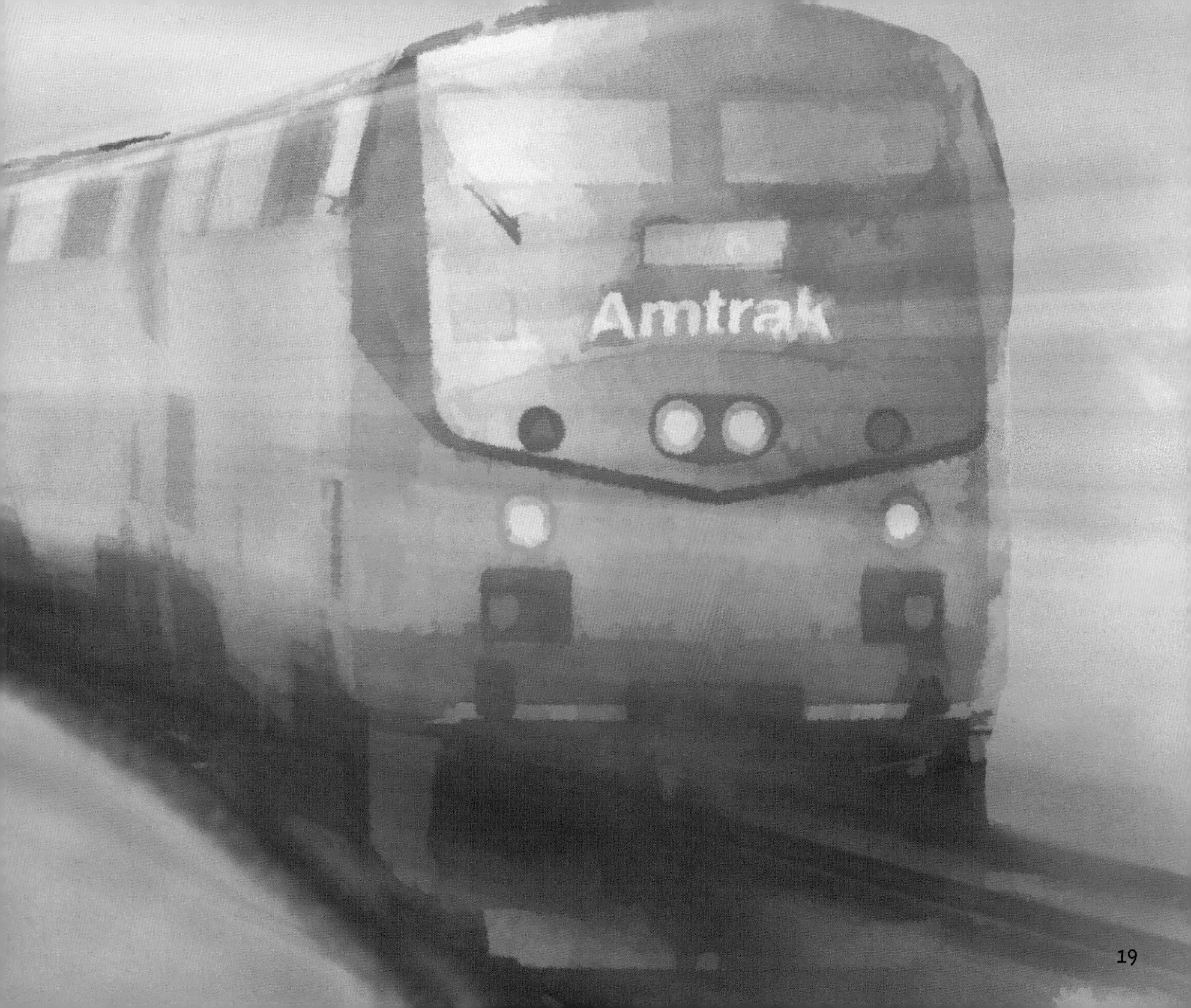
Amtrak

It's OK to be afraid

He asked his father to take him on a small plane ride and he really liked it.

He went to a tall building with his mom and took the elevator all
the way to the top and back down–it wasn't that bad at all.

At the zoo, he was very brave. Yes, the spiders and snakes are very frightening but some of them could be pretty and cool too. Howard told himself, "It's OK to be afraid."

Next, he asked his neighbor to teach him how to be friendly with a dog. Playing with the friend's dogs was fun! He was scared at first but because he was brave he did it anyway!

SECRETARY

28

Howard had so much fun taking care of each fear that when the first day at his new school arrived, he had almost forgotten about it.

He met his new teacher, shook hands with the people at the office and cafeteria and smiled at all the new boys and girls in his class.

Howard felt great!
All the while he told
himself, "I am brave.
I was afraid but I did
it anyway!"

Howard B. Wigglebottom Learns about Courage
Suggestions for Lessons and Reflections

★ FEAR IS OUR FRIEND

The words to be scared, afraid or fearful or to have fear mean the same thing.

Do you know what it means? Fear is when something or someone makes your heart beat really fast, you feel kind of bad and ill and you want to walk away from it.

It is very normal and healthy to feel fear. Birds, animals, fish, children and grown-ups are fearful of something at one time or another.

Fear protects us from danger and helps our bodies prepare to fight or to run away. Fear is our friend!

There are two basic kinds of fear—the real and the make-believe.

- The real kind is the fear of something that can really harm us. We should listen to this fear; it is there to protect us, to make us pay attention and be very careful.

What are the things we should fear?

We should fear spiders, snakes, scorpions, cars and trucks, strange people, dogs and animals, fire, lightning, electrical outlets, knives, rough and deep waters, high places.... Can you think of anything else to add to the list?

Remember it must be something that can really harm us.

- The make-believe kind of fear is when we are afraid of something that can't really harm us, like fear of the dark, fear of the first day at school, fear of toilets, fear of loud noises... Can you think of more make-believe fears we can have?

What kind of fears did Howard have?

Howard had both kinds. Which ones were of the real kind? Can you tell?

What fears do you have?

★ YOU CAN'T BE BRAVE IF YOU DON'T FEAR

How can superheroes, soldiers, firefighters and little birds be so brave? Because they do what they need to do even when they feel scared.

People who don't feel afraid of anything can't really be brave. Remember, to be brave is to have fear and do what you need to do anyway.

Can you be brave too? Yes!

Start by making a list of the make-believe fears you have. Ask your teacher and other grown-ups at home to help you with your list. Just like everything else you want to be good at, you will need to practice.

- Notice how you will feel scared at first just by talking about it.

- Draw a picture of your fear, look at the picture several times, and then throw it away.

- Tell your self aloud what the worst thing that can happen is if you do what you are afraid of.

- Tell yourself what the best thing that can happen is if you do what you are afraid of.

- Tell your self aloud, "I am afraid but I can do it anyway," or, "I can do it," or "I am brave," several times every day for five days.

- Be patient and kind with yourself. If you are still afraid of something it means you need a little more time. Tell yourself, "It is OK to be afraid"

- Be patient and kind with other children. Don't call them bad names just because they are scared. Let them know, "It is OK to be afraid." Everyone is afraid of something one time or another.

Learn more about Howard's other adventures.

BOOKS

Howard B. Wigglebottom Learns to Listen

Howard B. Wigglebottom Listens to His Heart

Howard B. Wigglebottom Learns About Bullies

Howard B. Wigglebottom Learns About Mud and Rainbows

Howard B. Wigglebottom Learns It's OK to Back Away

Howard B. Wigglebottom and the Monkey on His Back: A Tale About Telling the Truth

Howard B. Wigglebottom Learns Too Much of a Good Thing Is Bad

Howard B. Wigglebottom and the Power of Giving: A Christmas Story

Howard B. Wigglebottom Blends in Like Chameleons: A Fable About Belonging

Howard B. Wigglebottom Learns About Sportsmanship: Winning isn't Everything

WEBSITE

Visit www.wedolisten.org

- Enjoy free animated books, games, and songs.
- Print lessons and posters from the books.
- Email the author.